Rabbits

Lori Dittmer

CREATIVE EDUCATION
CREATIVE PAPERBACKS

seedlings

Published by Creative Education and Creative Paperbacks
P.O. Box 227, Mankato, Minnesota 56002
Creative Education and Creative Paperbacks are imprints of
The Creative Company
www.thecreativecompany.us

Design by Ellen Huber; production by Dana Cheit
Art direction by Rita Marshall
Printed in the United States of America

Photographs by Alamy (Arco Images GmbH), iStockphoto (Bob_
Eastman, chengyuzheng, ChuckSchugPhotography, coramueller,
Dorottya_Mathe, GlobalP, jimmyjamesbond, Kikovic, Leoba, lex-
ukr, Ljupco, Oleksandr Lytvynenko, mauro_grigolio, Neil_Burton,
Oktay Ortakcioglu, Photocech, saje, vasiliki, Voren1), Shutterstock
(IrinaK, Volodymyr Plysiuk)

Library of Congress Cataloging-in-Publication Data
Names: Dittmer, Lori, author.
Title: Rabbits / Lori Dittmer.
Series: Seedlings: Backyard Animals.
Includes bibliographical references and index.
Summary: A kindergarten-level introduction to rabbits,
covering their growth process, behaviors, the backyard habitats
they call home, and such defining features as their long ears.
Identifiers: LCCN 2017051391 / ISBN 978-1-60818-974-8
(hardcover) / ISBN 978-1-62832-601-7 (pbk) / ISBN 978-1-64000-075-9 (eBook)

Subjects: LCSH: Rabbits—Juvenile literature.
Classification: LCC QL737.L32 D58 2018 / DDC 599.32—dc23

CCSS: RI.K.1, 2, 3, 4, 5, 6, 7; RI.1.1, 2, 3, 4, 5, 6, 7; RF.K.1, 3; RF.1.1

First Edition HC 9 8 7 6 5 4 3 2 1
First Edition PBK 9 8 7 6 5 4 3 2 1

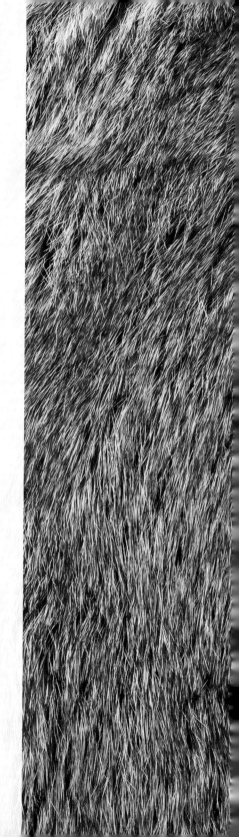

TABLE OF CONTENTS

Hello, rabbits!

Furry rabbits hop
through meadows.
They live in forests, too.

Some might be in your yard!

There are many kinds of rabbits.

Cottontails live in the Americas.

Some rabbits are
kept as pets.

Rabbits hear
with long ears.

Their big
eyes look
all around.

They thump their back feet on the ground to talk to other rabbits.

Rabbits eat plants.

They nibble grass, leaves, seeds, and tree bark.

Kits are born in cozy nests. At first, they do not have hair.

Rabbit mothers have many litters a year.

Speedy rabbits run from other animals.

They hide in the grass.

Goodbye, rabbits!

Picture a Rabbit

tail

ears

nose

eye

leg

whiskers

foot

Words to Know

kits: baby rabbits

litters: groups of animal babies born at the same time

meadows: lands that are mostly covered with grasses

thump: to hit something and cause a noise

Read More

Neuman, Susan B. *Hop, Bunny!: Explore the Forest.*
Washington, D.C.: National Geographic, 2014.

Zobel, Derek. *Rabbits.*
Minneapolis: Bellwether Media, 2011.

Websites

Easy Science for Kids: Rabbits and How They Are Different
from Hares
http://easyscienceforkids.com/all-about-rabbits/
Read more about rabbits, and watch a video of rabbits in the wild.

Enchanted Learning: Rabbits
http://www.enchantedlearning.com/themes/rabbit.shtml
Take a quiz about rabbits, read a rhyme, or make a rabbit puppet.

Index